PUEBLO STORIES

The
Basic Vocabulary Series

The books in the *Basic Vocabulary Series* are written with charm of style and high interest appeal for the children. Children love to read them for fun and thus get a vast amount of practice in reading skills. A high literary quality has been maintained in writing these true stories of animals, and retelling tales of folklore.

These Basic Vocabulary books are written with the Dolch 220 Basic Sight Words. The words make up two-thirds or more of all primary reading books and more than half of all other school books. The Dolch 95 Commonest Nouns have also been used. In addition to words from these two basic lists, each book has an average of about one new word per page.

This Series is prepared under the direction of Edward W. Dolch, Ph.D., Professor of Education, Emeritus, University of Illinois. The books in this series are:

Animal Stories	Lion and Tiger Stories
Bear Stories	Lodge Stories
Circus Stories	More Dog Stories
Dog Stories	Navaho Stories
Elephant Stories	Pueblo Stories
Folk Stories	Tepee Stories
Horse Stories	"Why" Stories
Irish Stories	Wigwam Stories

PUEBLO STORIES
IN BASIC VOCABULARY

By

EDWARD W. DOLCH
and
MARGUERITE P. DOLCH

Illustrated by

ROBERT S. KERR

GARRARD PUBLISHING COMPANY
CHAMPAIGN, ILLINOIS

Library of Congress Catalog Card Number 55-11203

Foreword

In the part of this country called the "Southwest," there are many tribes of Indians living in villages or pueblos. These pueblos are made of stone or of mud brick called adobe. Some of the pueblos are by the side of rivers, but most of them are on top of flat rock hills that the Spanish called *Mesas*, which means "tables." The most well-known of these Indians are the Hopi and the Zuni, but there are many others.

The Pueblo Indians live in what is called the "Land of Little Rain," but they raise corn and other foods by the streams, where some water is found. These Indians have been in this land for a very long time, and they have learned very much about raising food, making clothes, building houses, and so on. What they learned had not been written down before the white men came, but much had been kept in the stories which the old people told to the children.

Naturally, these Pueblo Indians have a great many stories about their past and about the world around them. These stories tell how things came to be and about the spirits that they believe in and pray to.

A few of the stories of the Pueblo Indians are given in this book. We hope they will show a true picture of these people and of their living. We hope that these stories will lead you to get some of the many books that will tell you more of these people, of their country, and of their life.

E. W. DOLCH

Urbana, Illinois

v

List of Pictures

Page

"These are my Nuts," said Ugly Boy_ x

The Bear Ran Away_____ 8

"You have what You Asked for,"
said the Bear _____ 16

The Boy Untied the Eagle's Leg_____ 26

The Boy was with His People Again_ 34

The Frog saw the Locust_____ 44

The Grandfather Made Arrows
for the Boys_____ 52

Only Part of the Leaf was Burned___ 60

The Coyote Showed his Teeth_____ 66

"Please Help me Get Ready," said
the Coyote _____ 78

The Turkey Girl was Sad_____ 86

The Turkey Girl Danced and Danced 96

They Stood Holding up the Rock____104

The Boy Put his Hand in the Hole__118

Sitting in the Kiva was a Magician___126

The Boys Ran from the Giant_____134

The Boy Could Hear the Water_____146

Tiyo Told about his Village_____154

Contents

Chapter   **Page**

1. The Ugly Boy _____ 1

2. Boy Not Afraid _____ 9

3. The Coyote and the Bear _____ 17

4. The Boy and the Eagles _____ 27

5. The Boy Gets Back _____ 35

6. The Frog and the Locust
   Sing for rain _____ 45

7. The North Star _____ 53

8. The Boys and the Star Man _____ 61

9. The Locust and the Coyote _____ 67

10. The Coyote and the Blackbirds __ 78

11. The Turkey Girl _____ 87

12. The Turkey Girl Goes to
    the Dance _____ 97

13. The Coyote and the Fox _____105

14. The Little Corn Bringer＿＿＿＿＿＿119

15. The Hummingbird Brings Rain＿＿127

16. The Giant of the Black Mesa＿＿＿＿135

17. Finding Rain＿＿＿＿＿＿＿＿＿＿＿＿＿147

18. The Snake People＿＿＿＿＿＿＿＿＿155

The Ugly Boy

Once there was a little boy who lived with his old Grandmother. He was not a pretty little boy. But his Grandmother loved him very much.

As the little boy grew up, he wanted to play with the other boys and girls. But he was so ugly that not one boy and not one girl would play with him. The children called him "Ugly Boy."

When Ugly Boy came by, the children ran into their houses. But Ugly Boy just laughed and went on about his work. And he had much work to do, for Ugly Boy was the only one that looked after the old Grandmother.

One day Ugly Boy said to the old Grandmother, "Grandmother, I am going to the Mesa and get us some piñon nuts to eat."

"No, no," said the Grandmother, "do not go to the Mesa. You know that there is a big Bear that lives on the Mesa. If the big Bear finds you, he will kill you."

"I am not afraid of any Bear," said Ugly Boy. "I go to the Mesa and I will bring back some nuts for you to eat."

All the people liked to eat piñon

nuts. But they were afraid to go to the Mesa to get them. They were afraid of the big Bear that lived on the Mesa.

All the people came and watched Ugly Boy go off to the Mesa. They thought that the big Bear would kill him.

Ugly Boy came to the Mesa. He sat down under a piñon tree and started to eat some of the nuts.

Ugly Boy heard something and he looked around. Coming at him was the biggest Bear that he had ever seen.

"Friend Bear," said Ugly Boy, "do not kill me. It will hurt you if you do. It will hurt you if you kill me."

The Bear had never had anyone talk to him like that.

The Bear sat down.

"Why do you say that it would hurt me if I killed you?"

"Just look at me," said Ugly Boy. "Did you ever see anyone that looked like I do?"

"No," said the Bear, "I have never seen anyone that looked like you."

Ugly Boy went on eating the nuts. And the Bear watched him.

Then the Bear said, "This is my Mesa. These are my piñon nuts. And you cannot eat my nuts."

"Friend Bear," said Ugly Boy, "you have many nuts. I came to get some nuts for my old Grandmother."

"You cannot have any of my nuts," said the Bear.

"They are not your nuts," said Ugly Boy. And he went on eating the nuts.

The Bear was very angry. "I will kill you. I will kill you," he said.

Then he looked at Ugly Boy. Ugly Boy did not look at the Bear. He just went on eating the nuts. The Bear did not know just what to do.

"Why did you say those are not my nuts?" asked the Bear.

"The nuts are for those who are not afraid," said Ugly Boy. "Friend Bear, I am not afraid of you and so these are my nuts."

"Ho, ho, ho," laughed the Bear, "we will see about that." And the Bear went off behind some trees.

Pretty soon the Bear came out from behind the trees. He was up on his back legs. And he growled as only a big Bear can growl. He ran at Ugly Boy.

Ugly Boy was not afraid. He just went on eating nuts.

The big Bear growled and growled. But Ugly Boy was not afraid. The Bear had never seen anyone that was not afraid of him. He had to give up.

"I can see that you are not afraid of me," said the big Bear. "But how can you make me afraid? And if you do not make me afraid, you cannot have any nuts for your old Grandmother."

Boy-Not-Afraid

Ugly Boy had been talking to the big Bear of the Mesa. The Bear could not make him afraid.

So Ugly Boy went back to his old Grandmother. And he sang a song as he went along:

> The Bear of the Mesa
> The Bear of the Mesa
> Shall be afraid of me
> Shall be afraid of me
> I know, I know,
> Yes, I know.

Ugly Boy sang the song over and over.

The people heard Ugly Boy singing. They came to see Ugly Boy. But Ugly Boy did not say anything. He went to the old Grandmother's house.

"Grandmother, bring the paint," said Ugly Boy. "Paint me as you have never painted me before. That old Bear is going to be afraid of me."

"All right," said the old Grandmother, "I will help you, for you are a good Boy. And you are not afraid of anything."

The old Grandmother painted

one side of the boy white, and she painted the other side of the boy black.

She painted red all around his eyes. And she painted blue all around his mouth. And all of the time the Grandmother painted Ugly Boy, she sang a magic song:

> Red and White
> And Blue and Black
> Never have you seen
> Never have you seen
> Black and White
> Red and Blue
> Ugly Boy will look at you
> Ugly Boy will look at you.

Then the old Grandmother gave Ugly Boy a magic stick.

"Go," she said. "See what you can do. You are a good Boy and you are not afraid of anything, of anything at all."

Ugly Boy ran back to the Mesa. He got behind a tree. Pretty soon the big Bear came by. He sat down under the tree and started to eat nuts. Then the Boy hit the tree with the magic stick. Down came the tree on top of the Bear.

Ugly Boy jumped out at the Bear.

"Hi, hi, hi, hi, hï, hi, hi, hi, hi," he sang.

The Bear took one look at Ugly Boy. The Bear had never seen anything like this. It was all white on one side, and all black on the other side. It had red eyes and a blue mouth.

The big Bear was very much afraid. He ran away as fast as he could go. He ran away from that Mesa. And he never came back.

Ugly Boy took as many nuts as he wanted. He took the nuts back to the old Grandmother.

"Grandmother," said Ugly Boy, "the Bear had too many nuts. He would not let the people have any of the nuts. But now the Bear has gone away from the Mesa. The people can have all of the nuts that they want.

The Grandmother washed the paint off Ugly Boy. She washed off the white paint, and she washed off the black paint. She washed off the red paint and she washed off the blue paint.

And when all the paint was washed off, Ugly Boy was not ugly any longer. And the children did not call the boy Ugly Boy any longer. They called him Boy–Not–Afraid.

Boy–Not–Afraid grew up and

all the people wanted him to be chief of the Pueblo. And he was never afraid of anything. The people were very happy, for now they could have all the piñon nuts they wanted.

The Coyote and the Bear

Once upon a time the Coyote and the Bear were friends. One day they were sitting talking together.

"Friend Coyote," said the Bear, "how would you like to plant a garden with me? We could plant the garden together. We could look after the garden together. We could divide what grows in the garden. Then when the cold wind comes we would both have much to eat."

"Friend Bear," said the Coyote, "I would like to plant a garden with

you. We will plant the garden together. We will look after the garden together. But how will we
divide what grows in the garden?"

"Well," said the Bear, "There is
the part of the garden that grows
on top of the ground. And there is
the part of the garden that grows
under the ground. Friend Coyote,
which part of the garden would
you like to have?"

The Coyote was always trying
to get the best of everything. But
he did not know very much about
gardening. However, he knew that
the Bear was always digging in
the ground for things that he liked

to eat. The best things in the garden must be under the ground.

And so the Coyote said, "Friend Bear, you take the part of the garden that grows on top of the ground. And I will take the part of the garden that grows under the ground."

The Bear went and got some corn to plant in the garden. He knew the Coyote did not know anything about how corn grew. The Bear thought that he would play a trick on the Coyote who was always trying to play a trick on others.

The Bear and the Coyote planted

the corn together. The Sun and the Rain helped the corn to grow. And pretty soon it came time to divide the corn.

The Bear took that part of the corn that grew on top of the ground. He carried it to his house. His wife was very happy to have so much good corn to eat. The Bear and his wife laughed at the Coyote who had asked for that part of the garden that grew under the ground.

When the Coyote came to get his corn, he began to dig in the ground. But he could find nothing that he could eat.

Then he went to the Bear and said, "Friend Bear, we planted the garden together. And we looked after the garden together. But now I have no corn that I can eat."

"Friend Coyote," said the Bear, "did you not ask for that part of the garden that grew under the ground?"

"Yes," said the Coyote, "I did."

"Do you have that part of the garden that grew under the ground?" asked the Bear.

"Yes," said the Coyote, "I do."

"Then you have that which you asked for," said the Bear.

And the Bear went into his house and went to sleep.

Some time after this the Bear said to the Coyote, "Friend Coyote, how would you like to plant a garden with me?"

The Coyote said, "Friend Bear, I would like to plant a garden with you. But when we divide I will take the garden that grows on top of the ground."

"All right," said the Bear.

And the Bear went to the store and got some potatoes to plant in the garden. He knew that the Coyote did not know anything about how potatoes grew. The

Bear thought that he would again play a trick on the Coyote who was always trying to play a trick on others.

The Coyote and the Bear worked together. They planted the potatoes together. They looked after the potatoes together. The Sun and the Rain helped the potatoes to grow. And pretty soon it came time to divide the potatoes.

The Coyote took all that was in the garden that grew on top of the ground. He carried it to his house. He and his wife looked and looked. But they could find nothing that they liked to eat.

Then the Coyote's wife was very angry.

"Go, and get me something good to eat," said the wife. "And if you do not find me something good to eat, never come back.

The Coyote went back to the garden. There was the Bear digging in the ground. He was digging up the good potatoes.

"Friend Bear," said the Coyote, "we planted the garden together. We looked after the garden to-gether. But now I have no po-tatoes that I can eat."

The Bear said, "Friend Coyote, did you not ask for that part of the garden that grows on top of the ground?"

"Yes, I did," said the Coyote.

"Do you have that part of the garden that grew on top of the ground?" asked the Bear.

"Yes," said the Coyote, "I do."

"Then you have that which you asked for," said the Bear.

The Bear carried his potatoes to his house. His wife was very happy to have the good potatoes to eat. And the Bear laughed at the Coyote who was always trying to get the best of everything.

And from that day to this, the Coyote will not talk to the Bear.

The Boy and the Eagles

At one time, there lived in a Moqui village an old man and an old woman. They had two children, a boy and a girl.

The Boy had an Eagle that he loved very much. The Boy was a good hunter. Every day he hunted rabbits. And every day he brought rabbits to his Father and Mother. But he always gave the biggest rabbit to his Eagle.

One day he said to the Girl, "Today I am going as far as the far mountain to hunt for rabbits. I shall be gone a long time. Please look after my Eagle today and give him food so that he will not get hungry. I have put a rabbit for him by the door."

The Boy went off to the far mountain to hunt for rabbits.

When the Girl gave the rabbit to the Eagle, she said, "Eagle, I do not like you. The boy loves you better than he loves me. He put a rabbit by the door for you. But he did not put a rabbit by the door for me to eat."

The Eagle was angry at the Girl. He could not help it if the Boy loved him better than the Girl. The Eagle would not eat the rabbit. And when the Sun was going down, the Girl brought the Eagle some bread. But the Eagle would not eat the bread that the Girl had given to him.

The Boy came to his house in the night. In the morning he went to see if his Eagle was all right. He saw the rabbit that the Eagle had not eaten. He saw the bread that the Eagle had not eaten.

"My Eagle," said the Boy, "you did not eat anything when I was gone."

"I do not want to stay here any longer," said the Eagle. "I do not want to stay where people do not love me. I want to go back to the Sky-Country where the Eagles live."

"But I love you very much," said the Boy. "I want you to always stay with me."

"The Girl does not love me," said the Eagle. "Untie my leg and let me go back to the Sky-Country and I will take you with me."

The Boy had always wanted to go up into the Sky-Country. And so he untied the Eagle's leg.

"Get onto my back," said the

Eagle, "and hold on. I will fly with you to the Sky-Country."

The Boy got on the Eagle's back.

"My Mother and my Father are working," said the Boy. "Let me tell them 'Good-bye'."

And so the Eagle flew over where the Father and Mother were working.

They looked up and they saw a big Eagle in the sky. And they heard a song.

My Father and my Mother
Good-bye, good-bye
To the Sky-Country
I fly, I fly.

As the Boy was singing, the Eagle was going up and up into the sky. The Boy could not see the ground at all. He was very much afraid.

"Please, my Eagle," said the Boy, "put my feet upon the ground again."

And so the Eagle flew to a big mountain and put the Boy down on top of the mountain.

"Stay here for a little time," said the Eagle. "I must be off to see my people. But I will come again to get you, for I love you very much."

Three days and three nights the

Boy stayed on top of the mountain. He was very hungry. But the Eagle did not come back to get him.

The Boy Gets Back

The Eagle had put the Boy on top of a mountain. For three days and three nights, the Boy stayed on the mountain.

Then the Boy started to walk down the mountain. He walked and he walked and he walked. And then he sat down.

The Boy heard someone calling. "Where are you going, my Boy?"

The Boy looked all around but he did not see anyone. Then he heard someone calling again.

35

"Where are you going, my Boy?"

"I am trying to find my friend, the Eagle," said the Boy.

"I will help you," someone said. "But first you must come into my house."

The Boy looked all around again but he did not see anyone. Then he saw a little hole in the ground, and he knew that it was the Spider-Woman who was calling him.

"I cannot go into the little door of your house," said the Boy.

"Yes, you can come into my house," said the Spider-Woman. "Put your foot on the door of my house and turn around three times."

The Boy put his foot on the little hole in the ground. He turned around three times. And then he fell into the house, or Kiva, of the Spider-Woman.

"You are hungry," said the Spider-Woman. "I will give you something to eat."

The Spider-Woman gave the Boy a little corn meal. The Boy ate all that he wanted. And there was a little corn meal left, for it was magic food.

"Go to sleep now," said the Spider-Woman. "And in the morning, I will help you to find your friend, the Eagle."

In the morning the Boy said to the Spider-Woman, "You have been very good to me. Now I will go out and hunt for you. I will get you many birds so that you will have much food."

This pleased the Spider-Woman very much. And she let the Boy go out and hunt for birds. And when the Boy came back with the birds, the Spider-Woman gave him a magic bag.

"Take this magic bag," said the Spider-Woman. "It will help you to find your friend, the Eagle.

Where the sun goes down, there is a road to the Sky-Country. No one can get into the Sky-Country without this magic bag."

The Boy thanked the Spider-Woman and started off to find where the Sun goes down. And when the Boy came to where the Sun goes down, he saw the road into the Sky-Country.

After a long, long climb, he came to the top of the road.

He looked all around him. And he saw that he was in the country of the Eagle People. Eagles were all around him. They came to him and talked with him.

"I have come to find my Eagle," said the Boy. "He left me upon the top of the mountain and he did not come back to me."

The Chief of the Eagle People called all of the Eagles to him. The Boy's Eagle came and he was very glad to see the Boy.

"Forgive me," said the Eagle. "When I came back to my people, I found my wife and children again. I forgot you and I did not go back to get you off the top of the mountain. Please forgive me."

"I love you very much," said the Boy to his Eagle. "I forgive you."

The Boy stayed a long time with

the Eagle People and he was very happy. But one day the Chief of the Eagle People said to the Boy, "My Boy, it is time that you go back to your people. Your Father and your Mother are old. You must help them. And the Girl cries for you."

The Eagle People gave the Boy many pretty things. Before the Boy left, the Chief of the Eagle People said to him, "Boy, My People are like Your People. They do not like to be tied up. Tell Your People never to tie up an Eagle. Let an Eagle fly up into the Sky-Country where his People live."

Then the Boy got on the back of his Eagle.

"Shut your eyes," said the Eagle, "and you will not be afraid."

The Eagle flew down, down, down. At last they came to the Moqui village. And the Boy was with his own people again. Then his Eagle flew off to the Sky-Country to be with his wife and children.

The Boy gave his Mother and his Father and his Sister all the pretty things that the Eagle People had given to him. He told the people of Moqui about the

Eagle People that live in the Sky-Country.

"They are like us," said the Boy. "They do not like to be tied."

And to this day people of that Moqui village never tie up an Eagle.

The Frog and Locust Sing for Rain

The Sun was very hot. The Clouds had all gone away. And no rain fell.

A Frog sat by a dry water hole. He knew that he would die if no rain came. And so the Frog made a song to the Rain Cloud.

> Rain Cloud
> I am little
> You may not see me.
> Rain Cloud, Rain Cloud
> Hear me, hear me
> Send the rain or I die.

The Frog sang his song again
and again.

But the Rain Cloud could not
hear the little Frog as he sang
by the dry water hole.

No rain came down.

By the water hole was some
dry grass. And on the dry grass
sat a Locust. He knew that he
would die if no rain came. And
so the Locust made a song to
the Rain Cloud.

Rain Cloud
I am very little
You may not see me.
I sit on the dry grass.
Rain Cloud

Hear me, hear me.
Rain Cloud
Send the rain
Or I die.

The Locust sang his song again and again. But the Rain Cloud could not hear the song of the little Locust.

No rain came down.

The Locust began to cry, for he knew that he was going to die. The Frog heard someone crying. He went over to the dry grass by the water hole. He saw the Locust sitting on the dry grass crying and crying.

"Friend Locust, are you crying because you are afraid to die?" asked the Frog.

"I do not want to die," said the Locust. "I want to sing. But I will die if the Rain Cloud does not send some rain to the earth."

"Have you made a song to the Rain Cloud?" asked the Frog.

"Yes," said the Locust, "I have made a song to the Rain Cloud, but I am so little that he cannot hear my song. And now I am going to die."

And then the Frog began to cry. He sat by the dry grass and he cried and he cried.

The Locust stopped crying and looked at the Frog.

"Are you afraid to die, Friend Frog?" asked the Locust.

"No, Friend Locust, I am not afraid to die," said the Frog. "But I do not want you to die. I want to hear you sing."

Then the little Locust tried to sing again.

"Let us sing together," said the Frog. "Maybe the Rain Cloud will hear us if we sing together."

The Locust and the Frog sang together. They sang a song to the Rain Cloud. They sang their song again and again.

Rain Cloud, Rain Cloud
Send down the rain
Send down the rain
We, the Frog and the Locust
We, the Locust and the Frog
We sing to you
Rain Cloud, Rain Cloud
Send down the rain
Send down the rain
Or we die.

The Rain Cloud up in the sky heard the Frog and the Locust singing together. The Rain Cloud filled the sky with black clouds. And the rain came down upon the ground.

It rained and it rained and it

rained. All the water holes were full of water just because the Locust and the Frog sang together.

The North Star

Once upon a time two brothers and their Grandfather were all that were left in an Indian village. They had been away from the village getting wood. And when they came back to the village there was no one there.

The old Grandfather and the two brothers went on living in the village.

One day the boys said, "Grandfather, please make us bows and arrows. We can hunt with them. Then we can get something for you to eat."

"I will make you bows and arrows," said the old Grandfather. "But first I must have the wood of the little tree that grows at the end of the village."

The Grandfather gave the boys a knife. Then the boys went to cut down the little tree.

The boys began to cut down the little tree. They thought they heard someone calling to them, "Please don't cut me. Please don't cut me."

The two little Indian boys looked around but they could see no one. Again they began to cut down the tree.

Then they heard someone crying, "Please do not cut me. Please
do not cut me."

The boys thought the tree was
talking to them.

"Please don't hurt me," said the
tree. "I am your Father. I have
been turned into a tree by magic.
Only you can help me."

"How can we help you? How
can we help you?" cried the two
little boys.

"Your Grandfather will tell you,"
said the tree.

The boys ran back to their
Grandfather as fast as they could
go.

"Grandfather, Grandfather," they cried, "the tree talked to us. It said it was our Father. Some magic has changed our Father into a tree. And our Father said that only we could help him. Grandfather, tell us what we can do to help our Father."

The old Grandfather sat and thought a long time. At last he said to the boys, "You will have to catch the Giant Star Man. He runs over the sky at night to get to his cave in the West. You must catch him before he gets to his cave. And if you do not catch the Giant Star Man before he gets into his cave, you, too, will be turned into trees."

Then the old Grandfather went to sleep in the sun.

The boys were very much afraid. They sat by their Grandfather until he opened his eyes.

"Grandfather," they cried, "tell us how to catch the Giant Star Man. We want to help our Father who is in the tree."

"You can try only once to catch the Giant Star Man. And I must make you ready," said the Grandfather.

"We will do anything that you ask of us," said the boys.

"Bring to me the heart of the little tree," said the Grandfather. "I will take the heart of the tree and make you bows and arrows. It is only with the heart of your Father that you can kill the Giant Star Man."

The two Indian boys went and cut down the tree.

"Father," they said, "we do not want to hurt you. But Grandfather says that he must have the heart of this tree to make our bows and arrows."

The Grandfather took the heart of the tree and made two bows. He made many arrows. And he showed the boys how to shoot the arrows.

One morning the Grandfather said to the boys, "You know how to shoot the arrows. Now I will make you ready to run faster than the Giant Star Man."

The Boys and the Star Man

The old Grandfather took a dry leaf from the corn. He lighted the end of the leaf.

"Now," he said, "you must run South to the other end of the sky. And then you must run back to me before this leaf burns out."

The boys ran South to the other end of the sky. And then they ran back to their Grandfather. But when they got back, the leaf was all burned out.

"If you want to catch the Giant

Star Man," said the Grandfather, "you will have to run faster than that."

The next day the Grandfather lighted another corn leaf. The boys ran to the East. They ran as fast as they could. They ran to the end of the sky and back. But when they got back, the leaf had burned out.

"If you want to catch the Giant Star Man," said the Grandfather, "you will have to run faster."

The next day the Grandfather lighted another corn leaf. The boys ran to the North. They ran as fast as the wind. They ran to the end of the sky and back again.

The Grandfather was very happy. For the boys were back just as the leaf burned out.

"In the morning," said the Grandfather, "you will run to the North again. But you must run faster than you did today. You must get back to me before the leaf has burned out."

The next day the Grandfather lighted another leaf. The boys ran to the North. They ran faster than the wind. They ran to the end of the sky and back again. And when they got back to their Grandfather only part of the leaf was burned.

"Now you are ready," said the

Grandfather. "Now you must catch the Giant Star Man before he gets into his cave in the West. Take your bows and arrows and shoot the Giant Star Man. Then you will stop the magic that holds your Father. But if you do not, the Star Man will turn you into trees."

The next morning, the boys got up before the Sun. They took their bows and arrows and ran to the big cave in the West. They ran so fast they got to the cave before the Giant Star Man.

The boys hid by the cave. They saw the Giant Star Man running like the wind. But before he could get into his cave, the boys had time to shoot their arrows. The Giant Star Man fell at their feet.

Then the two boys threw the Giant Star Man far into the sky to the North. And there he is to this day. We call him the North Star.

The boys went back to their Grandfather. And what do you think that they found?

All the people of the village had come back again. The boys' Father was sitting by the fire. And the old Grandfather was telling the Father that he had two boys who were not afraid of anything.

The Locust and the Coyote

Once upon a time an old Coyote lived with his wife and children in the rocks.

One day, the old Coyote went walking. He told his wife and children to stay at home. He wanted to go walking. As he walked in the sunshine he heard a Locust singing in a piñon tree. The Coyote stopped.

I sing, I sing, I sing.
I sing a song of sunshine,
I sing a song of rain,

I sing when I'm happy,

I sing when I'm sad.

I sing, I sing, I sing.

"What a pretty song," said the Coyote. "I would like to sing that song."

The Coyote sat down under the piñon tree.

"Friend Locust," he called, "you sing a very pretty song."

"I am glad that you like my song," said the Locust, and he went on singing, for he did not want to talk to the old Coyote.

"Help me to sing your pretty

song," said the Coyote. "Then I can sing the song to my wife and to my children."

The Locust knew that the Coyote would not go away until he had what he wanted.

"All right," said the Locust, "I will sing the song again."

I sing, I sing, I sing.
I sing a song of sunshine,
I sing a song of rain,
I sing when I'm happy,
I sing when I'm sad.
I sing, I sing, I sing.

"Now I shall sing the pretty song," said the Coyote.

The Coyote growled and howled and he thought that he was singing like the Locust.

"I sing very well," said the Coyote to the Locust. But the Locust did not say anything.

"Now I will go and sing this pretty song to my wife and to my children," said the Coyote. And he ran to his house as fast as he could go.

As the Coyote ran he growled and he howled. He thought he was singing the song just as the Locust had done.

An old Gopher who lived in the

ground saw the Coyote. "I will play a trick on that old Coyote," said the Gopher. "He is always trying to play tricks on me."

The Gopher made a hole in the ground. And as the Coyote came running by he put his foot into the hole and fell down.

The old Coyote growled and howled as he got the sand out of his eyes. He tried to catch the Gopher. But the Gopher ran into his hole in the ground. And the Coyote could hear him laughing.

"I do not remember my pretty song," said the Coyote. "I will have to go back to the Locust and ask him to sing his pretty song for me again."

The Coyote ran back to the piñon tree where the Locust was singing.

"I fell into a Gopher hole," said the Coyote, "and by the time I had got out of the hole and got the sand out of my eyes, I did not remember your pretty song."

"I will sing my song to you again," said the Locust. "See that you remember it this time." And the Locust sang his song for the Coyote.

I sing, I sing, I sing.
I sing a song of sunshine,

I sing a song of rain,
I sing when I'm happy,
I sing when I'm sad.
I sing, I sing, I sing.

"I know it now," said the Coyote. "I will go and sing the song to my wife and to my children." And the Coyote ran to his house as fast as he could go.

As the Coyote ran he sang the song of the Locust. He growled and howled. Some birds that were in the trees flew up into the sky. The old Coyote looked after them, and then he stopped.

"Oh, oh, oh," said the Coyote, "I do not remember my song. Now

I must go back to the Locust again."

The Locust thought that the old Coyote would not remember the song. He did not want to sing his song for the Coyote any more. And so he thought that he would play a trick on the old Coyote who was always playing tricks on others.

First the Locust took hold of the tree. And then he grew bigger and bigger and bigger. He was so big that his skin came in two parts right down the back. And then the Locust walked right out of his old skin and left it on the tree.

The Locust climbed down the tree to the ground. He found a little rock. He climbed up the tree and put the rock into his old skin. Then the Locust climbed down the tree and hid in the ground.

Pretty soon the old Coyote came running up to the tree and called:

"Locust, Locust, the birds in the trees flew up into the sky. Now, I do not remember your song. Friend Locust, sing your song to me again."

But the Locust on the tree did not sing the song.

The Coyote could see the Locust skin on the tree and he thought that it was the Locust.

"Locust, Locust, are you going to sing your song for me again?" growled the Coyote.

But the Locust on the tree did not sing the song.

Then the Coyote jumped up on the tree and he showed his teeth at the Locust.

"Sing your song again," growled the Coyote.

But the Locust on the tree did not sing the song.

The Coyote made a big jump. He bit the Locust skin. He bit so hard that the rock inside the skin hurt his teeth very much.

Oh, how that old Coyote howled and howled, for his mouth hurt very, very much. Then he got up and ran to his house as fast as he could.

The Locust climbed out of the ground. He climbed up into the tree. And he sang his song, for the Sun was shining and the Locust was very happy.

I sing, I sing, I sing.
I sing a song of sunshine,
I sing a song of rain,
I sing when I'm happy,
I sing when I'm sad.
I sing, I sing, I sing.

The Coyote and the Blackbirds

The Sun was shining and the Coyote thought that he would take a walk. And as he was walking along, he saw some Blackbirds. The Blackbirds were sitting in the top of a tree and calling out:

"Bring my bag. Bring my bag."

The Coyote thought that this was very funny. For why would Blackbirds want a bag? And so the Coyote went up to the tree and called to the Blackbirds:

"Blackbird Friends, why do you want a bag?"

"Have you not heard?" asked the Blackbirds.

"Heard what?" asked the Coyote.

"There is to be a big hail storm," said the Blackbirds. "Soon hail as big as eggs will fall from the sky. We are getting ready so that the hail will not kill us."

"Oh, oh, oh," said the Coyote, "I must get ready, too. I do not want the hail to hurt me,"

"Go and get a bag and a rope," said the Blackbirds. "We will help you get ready for the big hail storm."

The Coyote ran and got a big bag and a rope. He ran back to the tree where the Blackbirds were.

"Blackbird Friends," said the Coyote, "I have a bag and a rope. Will you please help me get ready for the big hail storm?"

"Friend Coyote," said the Blackbirds, "get into the bag. We will tie the rope to the bag. We will pull the bag up into the tree. And then when the hail as big as eggs comes it will not hurt you."

The Coyote got into the bag. The Blackbirds tied the rope around the bag. And then they put the rope up into the tree. They pulled and they pulled. At last they got the bag with the Coyote in it up into the tree.

The Blackbirds flew down to the ground. They picked up many little rocks. And all the time they were calling: "Oh, oh, oh, the hail is coming down. The hail is coming down."

The Blackbirds threw the rocks at the big bag up in the tree.

"Oh, oh, oh," cried the Coyote, as the rocks hit the bag, "this is a very big hail storm."

The Blackbirds threw more and more rocks at the Coyote. And all of the time, they were calling to each other:

"Oh, oh, oh, this hail will kill us. This hail will kill us."

"Oh, oh, oh," cried the Coyote, "that one hit me right on the eye. I think that this hail storm will kill us all."

"Friend Coyote," called the Blackbirds, "do not be afraid. You are big. The hail will not kill you. But think of us. We are so little."

And the Blackbirds threw and threw rocks at the bag in the tree.

Pretty soon the Blackbirds got tired. Then they let the big bag, with the Coyote in it, down to the ground. They untied the rope from the bag. And then they flew up to the top of the tree.

The Coyote hurt all over. He could not move.

"Oh, oh, oh," cried the Coyote, "the hail just about killed me."

At last he got out of the bag and looked around. The Sun was shining. He looked on the ground but he did not see any hail around. Then he knew that the Blackbirds had played a trick on him.

The Coyote was very angry.

"As long as I live, I will hunt the Blackbirds."

And never from that day to this

have Coyotes been friends with the Blackbirds.

But when you hear the Black-birds in the trees, they are telling over and over the story of how the Coyote was almost killed by the hail. And they laugh and laugh and laugh.

The Turkey Girl

Once upon a time there was a Girl with no Father and no Mother. She worked every day for some people who lived in the village. She looked after their Turkeys.

Every morning the Turkey Girl took the Turkeys to the foot of the Red Mountain. And at the foot of the Mountain, the Turkeys found many things to eat in the grass. When the Sun was going down behind Red Mountain, the Turkey Girl took the Turkeys back to their Turkey house and shut them up for the night.

The Turkey Girl did not look very pretty as she took her Turkeys to the Mountain. Her clothes were old and dirty. And her face and hair were not clean. She had no one to talk with and so she talked to the Turkeys.

"Mother Turkey," said the Girl, "you look very pretty this morning. Did you sleep well last night?"

The big Turkey would say, "Gobble, Gobble, Gobble."

"Yes, yes," said the Girl, "you are telling me that the Rain came over the Red Mountain last night. I heard it, too. There will be many things for you to eat this morning."

The Turkeys would all say, "Gobble, Gobble, Gobble."

The Turkeys all liked the Turkey Girl, for she was good and kind to them. They always tried to do just what she wanted them to do.

One morning as the Girl let the Turkeys out of the Turkey house, she heard a Man calling in the village. The Man was telling all the people of the village to make ready for a big dance. In four days there was going to be a big dance in the village and all the people from all around would come and dance. They would put on their best clothes. Everyone would have a good time. And there would be many good things to eat.

The Turkey Girl had never been to a dance.

"Mother Turkey," said the Girl, "I wish that just once I could go to a dance. I wish that I had pretty clothes and pretty beads."

The Turkey Girl danced a little as she took the Turkeys to the foot of Red Mountain.

Every day for three days the Turkey Girl could see the people of the village making their clothes ready when she took the Turkeys to the foot of Red Mountain. And at night when the Turkeys were in their house, the Turkey Girl knew of the good things the people were cooking. The people in the village were getting ready for a good time.

On the morning of the next day, the Turkey Girl was very sad as she took the Turkeys to the foot of Red Mountain.

"Mother Turkey," said the Girl, "I wish that once I could go to a dance. I wish that I had pretty clothes and pretty beads. And just for once, I would like to eat all the good things that I want."

The big Turkey said "Gobble,

Gobble, Gobble."

But this time the Girl knew what the Turkey was saying to her.

"Girl Mother," said the Turkey, "do as I tell you and this day you will go to the dance."

"This day you will go to the dance," said all the Turkeys.

"Oh, I am so glad that we can talk together, Friend Turkeys," said the Turkey Girl. "But how could I go to a dance? I have no pretty clothes."

"Do as I tell you, Girl Mother," said Mother Turkey. "When the Sun is up in the sky, we will go to our Turkey house. You are to come inside the Turkey house with us. But do not shut the door."

They did just as Mother Turkey said. When the Sun was up in the sky, all the Turkeys went back to the Turkey house. And the Turkey Girl went inside with them.

"Take off your clothes," said Mother Turkey.

The Turkey Girl took off her old dirty clothes. The Turkeys took the clothes and danced upon them. And now the clothes were new and pretty. The Turkey Girl took warm water and washed in it and washed her hair. When the Turkey Girl put on the new clothes, she was as pretty as any girl in the village.

Then the Turkeys put out their tails and gobbled. As they gobbled, pretty blue beads fell on the floor of the Turkey house. Mother Turkey took the beads and put them together.

"Girl Mother," said the big Turkey, "you will have the prettiest clothes and the prettiest beads of any girl at the dance."

"Thank you, thank you, Friend Turkeys," cried the Turkey Girl.

"Now," said the Mother Turkey, "you must do as I say or no happiness will come to you."

"I will do just as you say," cried the Turkey Girl.

"Do not shut the door of the Turkey house, and remember us when you are dancing."

"Yes, yes," said the Turkey Girl, "I will remember."

"We love you and we wish you happiness," said Mother Turkey. "But do not stay at the dance too long. Come back before the Sun goes down behind Red Mountain."

"Yes, yes," said the Turkey Girl.

Then the Turkey Girl ran to the village as fast as she could go.

The Turkey Girl Goes to the Dance

The Turkey Girl was very happy as she ran to the dance. She had on pretty clothes. She was the prettiest girl in the village.

No one knew the Turkey Girl. The girls of the village came to her and said:

"Where did you come from? Your dress is very pretty and your beads are the prettiest that we have ever seen. Please let us put on your beads."

The Turkey Girl laughed, but she would not let them.

"I cannot let you put on my beads," she said. "My Friends, the Turkeys, gave them to me."

Then all the girls laughed, too, because they thought that Turkeys could not give her beads.

The men and women said:

"Who is this pretty girl?"

No one knew the poor Turkey Girl.

The women gave the Girl the best of the food. And the men all wanted to dance with her.

The Chief of the village came and took the Turkey Girl to the ring of dancers. Of all the girls in the village, the Turkey Girl was the best dancer. She was very happy. Her feet were light. And she danced and danced.

But as she danced, the Turkey Girl did not remember her Turkeys. The Sun was going down behind the Red Mountain. On and on the Turkey Girl danced.

At last the Turkey Girl saw that the Sun was behind Red Mountain and was going down, down, down.

Then the Girl remembered her Turkeys. She ran away from the dance. She ran away from the village. She ran to the Turkey house.

Now what had the Turkeys been doing?

The Turkeys had been very happy when they saw their Girl Mother go off to the dance. She looked very pretty in her new clothes and her pretty beads. The Turkeys knew that she would be the prettiest girl at the dance.

Then the Turkeys went to sleep just as if the night had come. And all the time the Turkey Girl was dancing, her Turkeys were asleep.

When the Turkeys woke up, they saw that the Sun was going down behind Red Mountain.

"Our Girl Mother will soon come back to us," said the Turkeys.

Pretty soon the Sun had gone

down behind Red Mountain and the Girl had not come back.

Then the Turkeys were very sad.

"Our Girl Mother did not remember us. Our Girl Mother did not remember us," said the Turkeys. The Turkeys were very sad.

"Let us go out of this Turkey house," said the Mother Turkey. "We will not stay with someone who does not love us and remember us in her happiness. Let us go and live on the Red Mountain."

Night was coming. The Sun was down. One by one the Turkeys went out of the Turkey house. They went back to Red Mountain.

When the Turkey Girl got to
the Turkey house there was not
one Turkey there. She could hear
the Turkeys singing in the night:
    Our Girl Mother,
    She did not remember us.
    Our Girl Mother,
    She did not remember us.
    She danced,
    She danced,
    She danced.
    Our Girl Mother,
    She did not remember us.
    Our Girl Mother,
    She did not remember us.
The Turkey Girl called to her
Turkeys. But the Turkeys did not

come back to her. They went to live on Red Mountain.

The Turkey Girl's clothes now were old and dirty. Her hair was not pretty and clean. And she had no pretty beads. She sat in the Turkey house and cried and cried. And never again did she see one of her Turkeys.

And now the people of the village have to hunt their Turkeys on Red Mountain. The Turkeys run away from them and will not come when they are called.

The Coyote and
the Fox

Once upon a time a Coyote was walking by a village. He could hear the people of the village getting the corn ready for cooking. The Coyote was hungry and he wanted some of the corn meal to eat.

But the Coyote knew that the dogs in the village would run after him if they saw him. They would kill him if he did not run away very fast. And so the Coyote sat down upon the sand and thought what he could do.

As the Coyote was sitting on the sand, Little Blue Fox came by.

"Ho, ho," laughed the Coyote. "Now I shall eat Little Blue Fox, for many a time he has played a trick upon me.

"Little Blue Fox," called the Coyote, "come and talk to me, for I am very sad."

"I cannot stop now," said Little Blue Fox. "I have work to do. If you want to talk to me, you will have to come and help me with my work. The Chief of the village has asked me to look after the chickens."

Now the Coyote liked to eat chickens very much. And so he went with Little Blue Fox. When they came to the Chicken House, Little Blue Fox sat down by the door. "How am I going to get away from the Coyote?" he thought.

"The people of the village are going to have many chickens to eat," said Little Blue Fox. "The women are going to cook them. If we look after the chickens, the Chief will give us all the chickens we can eat. Let us close our eyes and rest while we wait."

The Coyote shut his eyes and thought of all the good chicken that he was going to get to eat. When he opened his eyes again, Little Blue Fox was gone.

The Coyote was very angry.

"Little Blue Fox has played a trick upon me again," cried the Coyote. "I am going to eat him up when I catch him." And the Coyote ran after Little Blue Fox, who was not far away.

Pretty soon Coyote came up to Little Blue Fox.

"Now I am going to eat you," cried the Coyote.

"No, no, no," cried Little Blue Fox. "Not now. The dance in the village is just going to start. Let us go to the dance together."

Now the Coyote liked to dance very much.

"Yes," said the Coyote, "I will go to the dance with you."

The Coyote sat down and began to make his hair look pretty.

"Friend Coyote," said Little Blue Fox, "first I must see the Chief. I had better go up that little hill and look into the village. You stay here. I shall be right back."

"Little Blue Fox will not trick me now," thought the Coyote. "I will keep my eyes on him."

"All right," said the Coyote. "But do not forget to call me when it is time to go to the dance."

Little Blue Fox went up the hill. Then he went over the hill. And then he ran as fast as he could run.

At last the Coyote got tired of sitting there. He went up the hill. But he did not see Little Blue Fox anywhere.

The Coyote was very angry.

"Little Blue Fox has played a trick upon me again," cried the Coyote. "I am going to eat him up when I catch him." And the Coyote ran after Little Blue Fox.

As the Coyote was running, he heard Little Blue Fox calling, "Help, help, help! Friend Coyote, come and help me." And then Coyote saw Little Blue Fox with his head against a great big rock.

The Coyote ran up to Little Blue Fox and he said:

"Now I am going to eat you. Nothing that you say will help you. I am going to eat you right now."

"No, no, no, Friend Coyote. Do not eat me. This big rock is falling down. I ran to hold it up. And if you eat me now, the rock will fall down and kill us both. Come and help me hold it up."

The Coyote stood up and put his head against the rock. He did not want the rock to fall down and kill him. And there Little Blue Fox and the Coyote stood side by side holding up the rock.

After a long time, Little Blue Fox said:

"Friend Coyote, I want a drink. You hold up the rock and I will go and get us both some water. For pretty soon you will want a drink, too."

"All right," said the Coyote. "But do not play a trick on me or I will eat you up."

Little Blue Fox ran down to the river to get a drink.

Soon the Coyote was very tired. Night was coming. And Little Blue Fox did not come back with the water.

At last Coyote said, "I want water so much that I must go to the river."

The Coyote began to let go of the rock. He was very much afraid that it was going to fall down upon him. At last he gave a big jump and ran as fast as he could run. But when he looked back, the rock was just as it had been before. Then he knew that Little Blue Fox had played a trick upon him again.

The Coyote was very, very angry.

"Little Blue Fox has played a trick upon me again," cried the Coyote. "I am going to eat him up when I catch him." And the Coyote ran down to the river to get a drink of water.

When the Coyote got to the river, he saw Little Blue Fox sitting by the water.

"Now I will eat you up," cried the Coyote.

"No, do not eat me up," said Little Blue Fox. "You would like a cheese better than you would like to eat me."

"Yes," said the Coyote, "I like to eat cheese very much."

"Friend Coyote," said Little Blue Fox, "I just got a cheese from a man. And when I went to get a drink of water, the cheese fell into the river. I wish I could get someone who can swim as well as you can. You could get my cheese from the bottom of the river."

The Coyote looked into the river. There he saw a big yellow cheese right in the river. The Coyote did not look up into the sky or he would have seen a big yellow thing in the sky that looked like a big yellow cheese.

Now the Coyote liked to eat cheese very much.

"I could never get your cheese from the bottom of the river," said the Coyote. "If I jumped in the river, I would come right up."

"I can tie some rocks to you so that you can go to the bottom of the river," said Little Blue Fox. "Then you can get the cheese."

"All right," said the Coyote. "I will get the cheese from the bottom of the river. But do not play a trick on me or I shall eat you up."

Little Blue Fox tied some rocks
to the Coyote. And then the Coyote
jumped into the river.

Down, down, down went the
Coyote to the bottom of the river.
And he never came out of the river
again.

The Little Corn Bringer

This is about a time when there was no rain. There was no corn to eat. The people had to go away to find food. And so they took all their things and moved away from their village.

A little Boy and a little Girl were playing together. They had gone far from the village. And when they came back their Mother and Father were gone. Their Grandmother and their Grandfather were gone. All the people in the village were gone.

The Boy and the Girl went into
their house and sat upon the floor.
They were very much afraid and
the little Girl began to cry.

"Little Sister, do not cry," said
the Boy. "I will make you a pretty
Bird. The little Bird will fly away
and find our Mother and Father."

The little Girl stopped crying.
The Boy went out and found a dry
part of the Sunflower plant. With
his knife the Boy made a little
Hummingbird. And when it was
done, the little Girl went to sleep
with the Hummingbird in her
hand.

Then the Boy took his knife and

went out hunting. He wanted to find something for them to eat. He looked to the East and he looked to the West. He looked to the North and he looked to the South. But not one thing did he find that he and his sister could eat.

After the Boy had gone, the little Girl woke up. In her hand was the little Hummingbird made out of the Sunflower plant.

"Pretty Bird," said the little Girl, "I am very hungry and I want my Mother. Please help me."

The little Girl threw the little toy away from her. Then right before her eyes, it was a Hummingbird and flew out of the door.

When the Boy came home, the little Girl told him about the Hummingbird. The Boy sat and thought a long time.

"Little Sister," he said at last, "this is good magic. The little Hummingbird that I made from the Sunflower plant will help us."

The Boy and the Girl went to sleep. When they woke up in the morning, the Sun was shining into the doorway of their house. Then what should fly through the doorway but the little Hummingbird.

The Hummingbird went right to a little hole in the wall. Then he went into the hole and the Boy and the little Girl could not see him.

The Boy got his knife. He made the hole in the wall bigger. Soon he could put his hand into the hole. The Boy found a little ear of corn in the hole.

The Boy and the little Girl cooked the ear of corn and ate it, for they were very, very hungry. As they were eating the corn, the Hummingbird came out of the hole in the wall and flew out of the door.

The Boy sang a song to the little Bird:

Fly, Little Bird,
Fly away.

Sun, the Father,
Will watch you.
Come again,
Little Bird,
Sun, the Father,
Will send you.

Then the Boy and the little Girl went to sleep.

When Sun, the Father, looked into the doorway the next morning, the children woke up. The first thing that they saw was the little Hummingbird who flew through the doorway and went into the hole in the wall.

The Boy went to the hole in the wall and put his hand into the hole.

He could tell an ear of corn was there, but he could not get it out of the hole. The Boy got his knife and made the hole bigger. Then he put his hand into the hole in the wall and pulled out a big ear of corn.

The Boy and his Sister cooked the ear of corn and ate, for they were very, very hungry.

And so it went on for five days. Every time the Boy had to make the hole in the wall bigger and bigger. For every day there was a bigger and bigger ear of corn in the hole in the wall.

The Hummingbird Brings Rain

For five days the Hummingbird had come through the door and gone into the hole in the wall. For five days the Boy and the little Girl had found an ear of corn in the hole in the wall.

Now the Hummingbird could not find any more corn. It flew and it flew. But nothing grew in the sand but cactus.

The Hummingbird came to a cactus with a big red flower on it. And under the cactus plant was a little hole. It was a very little hole but the Hummingbird could go through it.

The Hummingbird went down, down under the ground. At last it came to a big room called a Kiva, that was under the ground. And in this big Kiva was yellow corn and white corn. There was red corn and blue corn.

Sitting in the Kiva was a Magician. Many birds were flying about his head and talking to him.

"The people will die because they have no corn," said the Blue-birds.

"The corn cannot grow because

there has been no rain," said the Blackbirds.

The Magician just laughed and laughed.

"I put my magic upon the rain," said the Magician. "No rain can fall until I take my magic away."

The little Hummingbird flew to the Magician. It came to the Magician's ear.

"You should not put your magic upon the rain," said the Hummingbird.

"Who are you?" cried the Magician. "I cannot see you."

"I am little," said the Hummingbird, talking right into the Magician's ear. "But I have magic, too. You do not care if the men and women die. But did you think of the children?"

Then he told the Magician about the Boy and the Girl.

The Magician sat up.

"I had not thought about the little Boy and the little Girl," he said. "Take them an ear of blue corn from my Kiva."

The Magician let the Hummingbird take the biggest ear of blue corn that was in his Kiva.

When the Boy and the Girl woke up the next morning the first thing that they saw was the Hummingbird flying through the doorway of their house.

"Sister, Sister," cried the Boy, "our Hummingbird is back. He has gone into the hole in the wall."

And when the Boy put his hand into the hole in the wall, he found the biggest ear of blue corn that he had ever seen.

The Boy and the little Girl cooked the corn and ate it, for they were very, very hungry.

Then the rain began to fall.

The Hummingbird flew out of the door. It flew and it flew. It found the Father and the Mother. It found the Grandfather and the

Grandmother. It brought them back to the Boy and the little Girl.

The Boy told them about the Hummingbird that he had cut out of part of the Sunflower plant for the little Girl. And the Grandfather said:

"There is much magic in a Hummingbird. My Father told me that when I was a boy."

The Boy and the little Girl never saw their Hummingbird again.

But the rain fell on the ground all day. And the rain fell on the ground all night. The corn that was planted in the ground grew and grew. And before long there were big ears of corn to eat.

The people came back to the village. There was corn for everyone to eat.

The people made the Boy their Chief, for he was the one that brought the rain back.

But the little Girl is always looking for her Hummingbird.

The Giant of the Black Mesa

In the village, no children played upon the streets. All the men had gone to the Kiva. The Oldest Grandfather said to them: "Things cannot go on the way they have been going. Again and again the Giant of the Black Mesa comes into our village and takes one of our children away with him. And we never see that child again. Before long there will be no children in our village."

Then the Chief said to the men in

the Kiva: "We cannot kill this Giant with our bows and arrows. He is so big that our bows and arrows are just like playthings to him."

And the men in the Kiva said, "Yes, yes, yes, yes."

Then the Chief said to the Medicine Man:

"Make a Great Magic and kill the Giant of the Black Mesa."

The Medicine Man stood up and faced the North. He took a bit of corn meal from his medicine bag and threw it to the North. He turned to the East. He threw a bit of meal to the East. He turned to the South. He threw a bit of meal to the South. He turned to the West. He threw a bit of meal to the West.

"You may go now," said the Medicine Man. "I will talk to our people who have gone from us. When Sun, the Father, shows his face in the East, bring me some of the best and whitest corn meal in the village."

The men of the village climbed out of the Kiva. They looked at the Black Mesa that was far to the West. They thought that they saw the Giant putting wood into his big, big oven. The Giant was getting ready to cook his food. The men were much afraid.

The men went to their houses to see if all of their children were there. Everyone knew that the Giant liked to eat little boys and little girls better than anything.

When the men had gone, the Medicine Man had gone to sleep. When he woke up, he made a fire in the Kiva. He put some water by the fire. When the water was warm, the Medicine Man made a Great Magic over it. Then he went to sleep again.

When Sun, the Father, showed his face in the East, the men of the village climbed down into the Kiva. They brought the Medicine Man some of the best and whitest corn meal.

The Medicine Man opened his eyes and he said:

"I will do what our people who have gone have told me to do."

He took some of the magic water by the fire. He put it upon the white corn meal a little at a time. He mixed it and he mixed it. And all of the time the Medicine Man was singing a song of magic. With his hands, he made two little boys. He breathed on them and the little boys began to move. He breathed on them and the little boys began to grow.

Soon the little boys were as big as children. They ran around the Kiva and the Medicine Man talked to them.

The Oldest Grandfather told the little boys about the Giant of the Black Mesa, and how he liked to eat little boys and girls.

"We will kill him, we will kill him," cried the little boys. "We will kill the Giant of the Black Mesa."

For three days and three nights the men of the village stayed in the Kiva.

On the next day when Sun, the Father, showed his face in the East, the men carried the two boys out of the Kiva. The Medicine Man gave the boys magic bows and arrows. And the boys played up and down the streets of the village.

The Giant of the Black Mesa saw the boys playing in the streets of the village. With six big jumps the Giant was in the village.

The boys saw the Giant and ran away from him. But the Giant got the boys and put them in his big bag. With six big jumps he was back on the Black Mesa again.

The Giant put one of the boys in his red-hot oven.

"I will eat you when you are done," said the Giant.

The Giant went into his house and put the other boy into a little room that had no window in it. Then the Giant went to sleep on the floor.

As soon as the boy in the little room knew that the Giant was asleep, he took his arrow and hit the wall three times. At once a little hole was made in the wall. The boy jumped through the hole and ran to the oven. He hit the door of the oven three times. The door of the oven flew open and out jumped the other little boy. The hot oven could not burn the magic little boy.

"The Giant is asleep," said the first little boy. "Now is the time to shoot our arrows into his heart."

The two little boys ran into the house. They knew how to shoot their magic arrows into the heart of the Giant. Then the Giant of the Black Mesa was dead upon the floor of his house.

The two little boys ran back to the village. "The Giant of the Black Mesa is dead. The Giant of the Black Mesa is dead," they sang as they ran through the streets of the village.

The children ran out of the houses and played in the streets of the village again. The men and women of the village thanked the two little boys for killing the Giant of the Black Mesa. And all night long there were dancing and singing.

But just before Sun, the Father, showed his face in the East, the

Medicine Man took the two little
boys down into the Kiva. He made
a Great Magic and the two little
boys became white corn meal on
the floor of the Kiva.

Finding Rain

The Rain did not fall. The corn turned yellow. And the people in the village were very, very hungry. The women cried, and some of the little children died.

Tiyo, a man in the village, heard the women and children crying. He thought:

"I must find the Rain or all my people will die." And so Tiyo made a song to the Rain:

Rain.

Where are you?

Rain.

Where do you live?

Rain.

My people are hungry

Rain.

Where do you live?

Rain.

I go to find you.

Rain.

Where do you live?

Rain.

Where are you?

Rain.

Where do you live?

When the people of the village heard that Tiyo was going out to find the Rain, they said:

"Tiyo, Tiyo, do not go. Do not go. No one has ever been to where the Rain lives. You will never find the Rain. And you will never get back to the village."

But Tiyo was not afraid.

"I think that Rain must live on the other side of the Red Mountains," he said. "I will find where Rain lives. I will ask Rain to come back to our village. If Rain does not come, we all will die."

In the morning Tiyo left the village. He had his bow and arrows to hunt with. The people of the village did not think that they would ever see him again.

It took Tiyo many days to walk to the Red Mountains. For many days Tiyo climbed over the Red Mountains. Up and up he climbed. At last he saw what no one of his village had ever seen before. He saw the other side of the Red Mountains.

Tiyo put his hands to his eyes so that he could see better. He looked down, down, down, into a cut in the ground. And at the bottom of the big cut he could hear the water running. It was running fast and singing as it went.

"Down in the big cut must be the Country of Rain," Tiyo thought.

Then for days and days Tiyo climbed down and down and down

into the big cut. At last he came to the bottom of the cut, and there the water was running very fast.

Tiyo was tired. He went to sleep on the sand by the river. When he opened his eyes, he knew just what he was to do. He must make a boat out of a tree and go down the river looking for the Country of Rain.

When the boat was done, Tiyo got into it. Down the river he went, faster than the fastest man could run. For days and days, Tiyo went down the river. At last he came to where the river did not go so fast. Tiyo got the boat to the sand at the side of the river and got out.

He was very tired and he went to sleep on the sand.

When he opened his eyes, he saw a woman who stood by him. Tiyo knew that it was the Spider-Woman that his Grandfather had told him about.

"Are you going to eat me, Spider-Woman?" asked Tiyo.

"No," said the Spider-Woman, "I am not going to eat you. I am going to help you, for you are a man who is not afraid. Come to my cave and eat."

Tiyo went with the Spider-Woman. She took him to her cave and gave him good things to eat.

Tiyo stayed with her many days. At last Tiyo said:

"Spider-Woman, you have been very good to me. I will not forget you. But I must go and find the Country of Rain. I must ask Rain to come back to my people or my people will die."

"I do not know where Rain lives," said the Spider-Woman. "But I know where the Snake People live. And I know that the Snake People always have Rain when they want Rain. We will go and ask the Snake People where Rain lives."

The Snake People

In Tiyo's village there was no rain. The people were very hungry. Tiyo had gone to find the Country of Rain so that he could get Rain to come back to his village. Far on the other side of the Red Mountains, he had come upon the Spider-Woman, and she had said she would help him find the Country of Rain.

Then the Spider-Woman made magic. She grew very small and as a little spider she sat by the right ear of Tiyo. She told Tiyo the way to go. For days and days and days Tiyo with the little spider by his right ear walked over the mountains. He walked on and on. He walked over the red and yellow sands. At last he came to the Country of the Snake People. The Snake People live under the ground.

"I will stay here," said the Spider-Woman. "And when you come out of the Kiva, I will show you the way back to your village."

The Snake People liked Tiyo and asked him to come into their Kiva. And when the Snake People were under the ground in their Kiva, they took their skins off and were just like people.

Tiyo told the Chief of the Snake People about the people of his village.

"The people of my village will die," said Tiyo. "They have little corn to eat. Rain has not come and the corn is turning yellow. I must find where Rain lives and ask Rain to go to my people."

"We keep Rain under the ground," said the Chief of the Snake People. "The Snake People make a Magic and Rain always does just what we tell him to do."

Then the Chief of the Snake

People told Tiyo the Magic for Rain.

"The men must sing many songs. Then the men must paint one part of their body white for the white clouds. They must paint one part of their body black for the black clouds. They must find the snakes that are on the ground and put upon them corn meal from the Medicine Man. The snakes will come back to the Snake People in their Kiva under the ground. They will tell us what you have told them. Do all these things that I have told you and Rain will come to the people of your village."

Tiyo thanked the Chief of the Snake People. He wished to go back to his village at once. But the Chief of the Snake People said:

"Tiyo, the Snake People like you. I will give you one of our women for your wife. By my Magic she will be a woman and never be a snake again."

In four days, the Spider-Woman showed Tiyo and his wife the way back to his village.

Tiyo told to his people all that the Snake People had told him. They must paint their bodies just as they had been told to do. They must find the snakes and put on them the corn meal from the Medicine Man. Then they must let the snakes go back to the Snake People.

The people of the village did all these things. Then the Rain came. And ever after, when they did the right things in the right way, the Snake People would bring Rain to them again.

Tiyo was very happy with his wife. The people made him their Chief. And he lived happily a very long time.

And always his people remembered to do as he had told them.